THE SILVE

A delightful river romp featuring four swans, three children and one *egg*centric old lady!

Vivien Alcock has written many stories for children, including *The Cuckoo Sister* and *The Monster Garden*. "I write for children because, most of all, I enjoy telling stories," she says. "I like to write about strange happenings – ghosts or secrets or misunderstandings – in an everyday setting, in which nothing may be quite what it seems." As you will discover, there are certainly some very strange happenings in *The Silver Egg*! Vivien Alcock lives in London.

The
Silver Egg

Written by
VIVIEN ALCOCK

Illustrated by
IVAN BATES

WALKER BOOKS
AND SUBSIDIARIES
LONDON • BOSTON • SYDNEY

To my granddaughter Jessica
with love

First published 1997 by Walker Books Ltd
87 Vauxhall Walk, London SE11 5HJ

This edition published 1997

2 4 6 8 10 9 7 5 3 1

Text © 1997 Vivien Alcock
Illustrations ©1997 Ivan Bates

This book has been typeset in Plantin Light.

Printed in England

British Library Cataloguing in Publication Data
A catalogue record for this book
is available from the British Library.

ISBN 0-7445-5401-2

CONTENTS

Three children were walking along the river path.

CHAPTER 1

Day after day, hour after hour, a swan called Mirabelle sat on her empty nest and sighed. It was egg-time. The sun was shining. The river sparkled. Everybody else was happy.

Only Mirabelle was sad. Mirabelle had no eggs.

Mirabelle sighed again and looked down river, to where her sister Sophie sat on her nest. Sophie had eggs now, but she wouldn't tell Mirabelle where she had got them from. She just sat on them like a giant meringue on a plum pie.

I hope they all crack! Mirabelle thought.

The two large reedy nests were within

sight of each other low down on the river-bank. Set on the higher ground by the path, there was a bench on which an old woman sat, wearing a bunchy black dress, grey stockings and big black shoes. As usual, she was knitting, holding her hands low and not looking at what she was doing. In her lap there was a feathery little pile of dropped stitches and grey wool.

The swans had once tried to eat the grey wool.

Firmly, she'd shooed them away. So now they ignored her. She was there every day, part of the scenery, like a tree or a bush.

Three children were walking along the river path: a tall boy with his hands in his pockets, a small boy with big round eyes and their sister Kitty, who wanted them to listen to her.

"That lady's there again," she whispered. "Do you know what people call her?"

"No," Jake said, sounding cross and bored.

He was the tall one, who wished his mother realized he had better things to do in the holidays than look after Kitty and William. Just because he was a lot older than they were. "I know I can trust you, love," she said, whenever she was busy.

And she could, of course, but he wasn't going to pretend to like it. So he walked with Kitty and William as if he didn't belong to them. Let them chatter together and leave him to his serious thoughts about cricket and computers.

"They call her the swan lady," Kitty said, trying to attract his attention.

"Why?" William asked. He was always asking why. "Why is jam sticky?", "Why is grass green?" and now, "Why are you pinching me, Kitty?"

"To shut you up." Kitty turned to her older brother. "Why do you think they call her the swan lady, Jake?" He shrugged.

"Dad says she's an eccentric – "

"What's an egg-centric?" William asked.

"Shut up, William. Don't talk so loud. She'll hear you," Kitty whispered, and then went on. "Dad says she comes here every day when the swans are nesting. She brings her lunch and her tea in her knitting bag, and her big umbrella. Do you know why she always brings her big umbrella?"

"In case it rains?" William suggested.

"No," Kitty said. "Jake, can you guess?"

Jake was fed up with Kitty and her showing-off. "So she can hit people with it," he said.

"Did Dad tell you too?" she cried, looking

so crestfallen that he had to laugh.

"No. I guessed. Does she really hit people?"

"Not just anybody. Dad said some brainless louts used to throw stones and bottles at the swans' nests, breaking the eggs. Then they ran off before anyone could catch them. That's when she started coming."

"I hope she hit them!" William said fiercely.

Kitty smiled. "Dad saw her once, chasing five smelly hooligans. He said he'd never seen a more terrifying sight. Her mouth was wide open, her face crimson with fury, and all the time her umbrella was going *thwack! thwack! thwack!*"

"Good for her," Jake said, forgetting to be bored.

William clapped his hands and cheered. Too loudly.

The swan lady turned her head and stared at the three children. Her eyes were small and bright under frowning black eyebrows. She did not say anything, but Kitty was suddenly afraid.

"Come on," she muttered. "Let's go!"

"Why?" asked William.

"Because I say so. Let's go and have a look at those swans in the reeds over there."

"Keep away from the swans when they're nesting!" the lady said sharply. She fixed them with her cold bright gaze. "They'll attack you if you go too near. Break your arms like matchsticks. And serve you right."

"Why?" William asked. "We wouldn't hurt them."

William's eyes were big and blue. "Baby-eyes," Jake called them.

The lady's face softened a little. "How are they to know that? Can you tell them? Can you speak their language?"

"They haven't got a language," Kitty informed her. Kitty was the clever one. She liked telling people things. "Dad says they're called mute swans and mute means dumb."

"It's a pity know-it-all girls aren't mute," the swan lady snapped. "And you're wrong. Mute swans can hiss and snort and honk. Listen! The one on that nest over there is hissing now."

"Why?" William asked.

"She is sad. Can you hear her now? Hissing and sighing, hissing and sighing."

"Why?"

"She is complaining because it is egg-time and she has no eggs. No eggs, no babies. Don't ask me why she wants kids," the swan lady said. "Kids are nothing but trouble. Ask too many questions. Go away now. Shoo!"

She turned on them fiercely, with her

round eyes flashing and her words snapping out.

Startled, Jake and Kitty ran off down the path. Then Jake went back for William, who hadn't moved.

"Come on," he commanded, grabbing William's hand and pulling him along. Kitty, coming to meet them, peered into William's face. "You're not crying, are you?"

"Not exactly," he said. "I was just thinking about that poor sad swan without any eggs."

She laughed. "Oh, William, you're such a softie! Forget it. There's nothing we can do about it. No good giving her our breakfast egg."

"Why not?"

"Too small," said Kitty, who always knew everything. "Swans' eggs are this size." She stretched her thumb and forefinger apart as far as they would go. "Or bigger."

William thought of his last Easter egg. His mother was saving it for him in the fridge. A beautiful egg, just the right size. A chocolate egg covered in bright silver paper and tied with a green ribbon.

I'll give it to her, he thought. *I'll think of a way. And I won't tell Jake or Kitty because they'd only tell me not to be silly. They think I'm silly because I'm the youngest, but I'm not.*

He walked home between Jake and Kitty, smiling to himself, and dreaming of a happy swan.

I'll do it tomorrow, he thought.

"No eggs. Got no eggs. S'not fair."

CHAPTER 2

Mirabelle was still sighing and complaining.

"No eggs. Got no eggs. S'not fair."

Her husband sighed too, feeling it must be his fault. Everything was always his fault. Like the untidy nest they'd built last year, which had slipped down into the moonlit river one night, dunking poor Mirabelle into cold water in the middle of a happy dream.

What a fuss she'd made, kicking and hissing and hooting, and beating up the water with her wings. She'd woken all the other birds, making them cross. Very cross. Especially her sister Sophie.

It had all been his fault for bringing her the wrong sort of sticks and reeds. "Nobody could have made a proper nest out of them," she'd said.

Then there was the strange long-legged insect he had brought for her breakfast yesterday morning that had turned out to be a piece of tangled thread that nearly choked her.

He had got hold of one end of the thread with his beak and pulled. Mirabelle had dug her heels into the mud and pulled the other way. The thread had grown longer and longer until suddenly, out it had come and they'd both fallen down.

All the other swans had laughed. Especially Mirabelle's sister Sophie.

"Never mind, dear," Egbert had said. "Don't take any notice of her."

But Sophie was so big and fat and smug, it

was difficult not to see her out of the corner of your eye, wherever you looked.

Egbert was a kind swan, but not clever. He did his best but his best was never good enough. He sat beside Mirabelle now, as she sighed on her empty nest, and said things like, "There, there. Don't worry. Better late than never."

"Supposing it is never?" she asked gloomily. "Every night I pray for a feathered angel to bring me an egg. Just one. I'm not greedy like some people I know. But every morning when I wake, what do I see? Nothing."

She arched her long neck and wiped her eyes on her wing.

"Perhaps tomorrow," Egbert said.

"Tomorrow and tomorrow and tomorrow," she grumbled. "I've heard that before. Every day is yesterday's tomorrow. And still I haven't got an egg. While she, she over there – " Mirabelle turned her head and glared up the riverbank to where her sister Sophie spread herself over her beautifully made nest like a giant cotton duvet. "Seven! That's what she's got! What does she want with seven? She can't even count."

"Never mind, my dear," Egbert said.

"She was always stupid," Mirabelle grumbled. "I was the clever one of our lot, not her. Last to hatch out, she was. Now see the airs she gives herself. See how smug she looks, preening herself as she sits on her seven eggs. You did say you saw seven?"

"I think so. I'm not sure. It might have been six."

"Might have been six," Mirabelle repeated thoughtfully.

Suddenly her eyes brightened. An excited ripple ran up and down her long bendy neck. "Egbert! You're a *genius*!"

"Am I, my dear?" he asked, pleased but bewildered. "Are you sure you've got the right swan? Do you really mean *me*?"

"Of course I mean you. Who else could I mean?' She bent her neck and hissed softly into his ear. "So when are you planning to do it?"

"Do what?"

"Steal one of her eggs, of course!"

"*What!*"

"Sssssh!" she whispered.

They both looked up the riverbank to where Sophie sat snoozing over her seven eggs.

"She'll never notice," Mirabelle went on. "Four, six, three, seven, five – it's all the one to her. Just rearrange the eggs in the nest so there isn't a gap and she'll be none the wiser."

"But how can I do it? She sits on her nest

like a saucepan lid all day, and even when she leaves it for a moment, Hector takes over."

Hector was Sophie's husband, a big, strong, heroic swan. A good husband, if you like them thick in muscle and thick in the head. But a horrible fierce enemy. Three times already, over some mild squabble, Egbert had had to bow his neck humbly to Hector's punishing beak.

"He hits really hard, even over little things," he complained. "If I steal one of their eggs, he'll kill me, Mirabelle. He's never forgiven us for building our nest too near to his."

"How do you mean 'too near?' We're family, aren't we?"

"That won't stop him. He's never liked me. He'll tie knots in my neck. I know he will."

"Hush, my dear. As if I'd let you do it if there was any danger. I'll think of a plan. You know how clever I am. We'd better not leave it too late. We'll do it tomorrow."

"Tomorrow?" he honked weakly, and would have turned pale if he hadn't been covered with white feathers already.

"Tomorrow," she said firmly.

*Mirabelle peered hopefully under
her fat, feathered tum.*

CHAPTER 3

Mirabelle was the first to wake. The mist over the river was pale and bright. Soon the sun would be up. She lumbered to her feet and peered hopefully under her fat, feathered tum. No egg. She sighed, and poked Egbert with her beak.

"Hey! What?" he grunted, opening his eyes. "Oh, hullo, dear. Is it time to get up already?" His head swivelled round on his neck. "Where's everybody? It's so quiet. Even those noisy hooligans in the trees haven't started up yet. Let's have another five minutes' snooze."

"No. Today's the day." Mirabelle looked

round carefully. The swan lady's bench was empty. There were no children on the banks. Sophie and Hector still slept in their nest up river. "Listen, and I'll tell you my plan," she said.

William was the next to wake. He slid silently out of bed and crept down to the kitchen. Nobody was about. He opened the fridge door and looked inside.

Where had his Easter egg gone? He couldn't see it. He knelt down and began taking things out and putting them on the floor: half a cold chicken, a packet of bacon, a packet of sausages, a round dish covered with tinfoil – what was it? Chocolate cream!

He began eating it.

"What are you doing, William?" his mother said, coming through the door.

"I was looking for my last Easter egg,"

William opened the fridge door and looked inside.

he told her.

"Well, that's not it, darling. That was supposed to be our pudding for tonight."

She took the bowl away from him, covered it again and put it back in the fridge. Then she opened the blue plastic drawer at the bottom.

"Your egg's in here with the salad things."

"Why?"

"I couldn't think where else to put it. Here it is. Don't eat it before breakfast. You'll spoil your appetite."

"I'm not going to eat it. I'm going to give it to a friend."

His mother smiled and kissed the top of his head. "There's my kind boy," she said.

"Don't tell Jake or Kitty, Mum, or they'll want some."

"I won't tell a soul," she promised.

He nearly told her that his friend was a swan, but perhaps she'd think him silly.

Perhaps she'd make him promise not to go near the swans when they were nesting. Perhaps she'd say, like the swan lady had, that they were dangerous and would break his arms like matchsticks.

Better not say anything.

He took the silver egg upstairs to his room and put it on his bed.

Then he took his magic book down from the shelf. *Magic Made Easy*, it was called.

William had already amazed his mother and father with the Obedient Orange. It had taken some practice before he could do it properly. When he was ready, he'd called everybody into the sitting-room, and made them all sit on the sofa and chairs facing him. He was already in position, standing behind the little table with the fringed velvet cloth.

When they were sitting down, and Kitty had stopped giggling, he began. Waving his hands over the orange, he'd chanted:

"Orange, orange, hear what I say!
Come when I call you. Orange, obey!"

Then he had backed away from the table, beckoning. The orange, after a little jerk, had moved slowly towards him…

Kitty jumped to her feet.

"He's got something under the cloth!" she'd cried, running forward. Before he could stop her, she picked up the orange and lifted the cloth away, revealing the curtain ring on the table, attached by a long dark thread to his belt. "See? When he backs away, it pulls the the ring towards him and moves the orange on top of the cloth. It isn't magic. It's only a trick!"

Then, seeing his face, she was sorry. She hugged him and added, "A very good trick, though. You are clever, William."

She hadn't quite spoiled it for him. It had been magic for a moment, the orange moving forwards and Mum and Dad smiling in amazement...

There was nothing about Obedient Chocolate Eggs in the book. Perhaps he could adapt the spell to fit. But he needed real magic, not a trick with curtain rings and thread. He sat and thought.

At last, he stood up. Stretching out his hands over the silver egg, he linked his thumbs together, and flapped his fingers up and down like wings, chanting softly:

"Silver egg, silver egg, do what I say,
Hatch into a silver swan. Hear and obey!"

The swan lady stared over a low bush.

Chapter 4

"Your plan won't work," Egbert said, shivering on his feet. "How can I frighten Sophie? *She* frightens *me*."

"I'll disguise you. I'll make you look horrible."

"She'll recognize me. I know she will. She'll tell Hector when he comes back from hunting, and he'll pluck all my feathers out."

"Never mind, dear. They'll grow again. It's getting warmer every day. You won't catch cold."

"How can you be so heartless, Mirabelle! The whole world will laugh at me."

He looked so distressed that Mirabelle felt

sorry for him. But what could they do? If they gave up her plan, there'd never be an egg in their empty nest, never.

"Please, Egbert. Dear kind Egbert," she said, entwining her neck with his. "I promise it won't come to that. Not if you do exactly what I say. Where is Hector now?"

Egbert unwound his neck from hers and looked over the tall reeds.

"He's looking for food by the wooden pole," he told her.

"He won't stay there long. Then he'll be off for his big hunt by the old boathouse. Now quick, we must get ready."

"Where are we going?"

"To the boggy black mud round the corner."

"What, now?"

"Yes."

"Supposing somebody steals our nest

while we're both gone?" asked Egbert.

Mirabelle looked at the ragged pile of reeds and twigs.

"They won't bother, dear," she said.

The swan lady came down the river path. She was wearing a small feathered grey hat today, and a brown dress, and she was carrying her big umbrella and her knitting bag in her hands.

Suddenly she stopped and stared over a low bush on the river's edge. Two swans crouched on the other side, on the edge of a patch of boggy black mud. Two swans whom she knew well.

What are they doing here? she wondered.

"Keep your neck straight and stand still," Mirabelle commanded.

"I can't. You're tickling me."

Mirabelle began to spread mud over Egbert's neck.

"Well, do your best."

Mirabelle dipped her beak into the oozy, squelchy, malodorous black mud. Like an artist with a palette knife, she began to spread it over Egbert's neck. When the sun dried the mud, it became a smudgy sort of grey, with little white freckles where flakes of mud had fallen off. "What do I look like?" Egbert asked.

"Quite pretty," Mirabelle told him.

"Aren't you going to do my body now?"

"I don't think I'll have time. Your neck needs a second coat. It's too pale."

"You said I could be a beautiful black swan."

"Well, you can't. You'll have to be a white swan with a smudgy grey neck."

"There aren't any white swans with smudgy grey necks!" he protested.

"There are now," she said.

She scooped up great dollops of the mud and patted it thickly on to his neck with her beak. Mud spattered his folded wings and speckled his chest.

"There, that's done," she said at last. "Keep still a moment and give it time to dry."

Egbert stood like a statue, the thick coating of mud on his neck baking in the sun.

"Tell me when I can move," he said.

"Just a minute." She arranged some dangling green weeds over his head like a mask. Then she washed her beak in the river, dried it carefully on the bush, and said, "You can move now. Look down at your reflection in the river."

After a pause, Egbert said, "I can't."

"Why not?"

"I can't bend my neck. The mud has dried

as hard as a chimney pot."

"Oh dear," said Mirabelle. "Well, at least if Hector catches you, he won't be able to tie your neck in knots. You must try and look on the bright side of things, my dear."

The swan lady walked on, puzzled by the swans' odd behaviour. She had never seen anything like it before. Was it some form of social grooming?

"Like my sister having a mudpack to improve her complexion?" she wondered, smiling. "Can't be. Swans have more sense."

When she came to her bench, she sat down and began planning a letter to *Country Life* magazine.

The children came walking along the river path.

CHAPTER 5

The children came walking along the river path, carrying bathing towels. They were going swimming, not in the river where the water was brown and green and smelled of mud, but in the bright blue Lido, where the water smelled of chlorine and there was a lifeguard sitting high up, watching the swimmers and chatting to the pretty girls.

Jake wore his towel thrown carelessly over one shoulder. Kitty wore hers round her neck, like a scarf. William's was rolled up neatly. He held it carefully, with one hand at either end, as if it contained something that might escape, given half a chance.

He was very quiet. Kitty thought he was disappointed because their mother couldn't come to watch him swim today.

"Tomorrow," Mum had promised, kissing him. "I'll come tomorrow without fail. All right?"

William had nodded, but he'd kept his head bent over his towel.

"Poor William," Kitty thought. "I bet he's going to cry."

She was wrong. William kept his eyes hidden because he didn't want his mother to notice he was pleased she wasn't coming with them today. His mother would have held his hand and probably wanted to carry his towel and ruined everything. It was bad enough that the swan lady was there again on her bench. Still, she was sitting with her back towards them, intent on her knitting. If he was careful, she wouldn't notice.

He craned his neck so that he could see over the tall reeds to the shallow, marshy edge of the river. Looking for the sad swan's nest.

"Why, it's empty!" he cried, catching sight of it.

"What is?"

"The nest. Do you think that poor swan's gone for good?"

"No," the swan lady said. At least that's what they thought she said. She didn't turn round to look at them as she spoke. She might have been talking to herself. Or just snorting to clear her nose.

They looked uneasily at the big umbrella propped up against the bench beside her and hoped she wouldn't mistake them for brainless louts.

"I think we'd better be going," Kitty said in a high, artificial voice. "I told my friends

I'd come early." They weren't meeting anyone in particular but she felt they needed an excuse for leaving.

She and Jake walked on.

William stayed where he was. This was his chance.

He slid the silver egg out of his towel. Nobody was looking at him now. He was a good shot. He tossed the egg in a gentle curve. It fell like a lopsided silver moon into the empty nest.

He smiled, thinking how pretty it looked. Then he turned to go after Kitty and Jake.

Someone was blocking his way. The swan lady towered above him, her small head jutting forward, her black brows scowling above her cold bright eyes.

"Got you!" she said, and raised her big umbrella.

"I only wanted to give the poor swan an

egg!" He cried. "Please don't hit me!"

"An egg?" She peered down into the nest and saw it gleaming in the sunlight.

William dodged past her and ran along the path, yelling for his brother and sister to wait.

She did not follow him, but instead stepped down to the nest and, reaching out a large hand, took up the silver egg.

Silly boy, she thought. Did he really think it would hatch?

But she was touched by his kindness. She carried the silver egg carefully, meaning to give it back to him when she caught him up.

Mirabelle made straight for her sister's nest.

CHAPTER 6

Mirabelle and Egbert were round the bend of the river, peeping through the reeds.

"Can you see Hector anywhere?" Egbert asked.

"No. He's gone."

"Are you sure?"

"Yes."

"Supposing he comes back before we've finished?"

"He won't. I'm off now. Remember, count up to seventeen eggs and then follow me."

"All right."

"Don't let me down, will you? Be brave,

my dear," Mirabelle said. Then away she went.

The people on the bank might have been trees for all the notice she took of them. She made straight for her sister's nest, honking and snorting, making as much noise as a mute swan could.

Sophie woke up.

"Go away," she hissed, puffing up her feathers threateningly.

"Sophie, it's me! Your sister Mirabelle – "

"I can see that. Go away, Mirabelle, or I'll call Hector."

"*Sophie!* I come to help you, my own sister, and this is the thanks I get!"

"Help me? You? That'll be the day."

"Have it your own way," Mirabelle said, shrugging her wings. "Only don't say I didn't warn you. He'll be here any minute."

"Who will? What are you talking about?"

"The green-crested, grey-necked, egg-eating monster – "

"Egg-eating?" Sophie whispered in horror.

"Yes. If I were you, I'd push my eggs onto the bank behind the nest where he won't see them," Mirabelle said. "He'll go away if he sees the nest is empty. However, please yourself. I don't suppose you want my advice."

It so very nearly worked. Sophie, confused and frightened, pushed one of the eggs onto the edge of the nest. Then she caught sight of Mirabelle watching it hopefully.

She paused. She remembered the tricks her sister used to play on her in the past. She remembered the time Mirabelle had persuaded her it was lucky to pluck the tail feathers of a brown four-legged thing sitting on the bank. "It won't mind," she'd said.

But the brown four-legged thing had

minded very much, and had shouted, "Rough! Rough! Rough!" and shown rows of sharp yellow teeth, frightening poor Sophie out of her wits.

"I don't believe you!" she cried now. "Green-crested, grey-necked, egg-eating monster indeed! There's no such thing, not even among the raggle-taggle winter visitors. Come on! Show it to me. Where's this amazing creature?"

"There!" Mirabelle told her triumphantly. "Over there!"

Sophie jumped round to look where her sister was pointing.

The swan's sudden movement shook the nest beneath her, and the egg balanced on the edge rolled over. Slowly, gently, it trundled away down the muddy slope and vanished behind some reeds.

Only the swan lady saw where it went. She

stepped carefully down the bank and picked it up. Now she had two eggs, one in each hand. They were much the same size. One was silver and cool. The other was greenish grey and warm.

About to slip this one back into its crowded nest, she hesitated. She thought of the young boy giving up his silver egg to comfort a sad swan. He wouldn't want it back. Surely he'd rather believe that his impossible dream could come true!

She smiled.

Pushing the chocolate egg into her big pocket and holding the other one carefully in both hands, she walked quickly back to the empty nest – *and very nearly missed seeing what was happening behind her until it was too late!*

A fantastic swan came round the bend in the river.

CHAPTER 7

A fantastic swan came round the bend in the river. His body, white and rather skinny, looked too frail to support his massive grey neck. This, stiff as a marble pillar, was topped by a tiny pale head with a quivering orange beak.

As he swam towards them, he swayed from side to side and seemed in danger of toppling right over. A gentle hissing came out of his beak.

"I am the fearsome green-crested, grey-necked, egg-eating monster," he whispered.

Rehearsing his part as he swam, he seemed unaware that he already had an audience. The green weed dangling over his eyes blinded him to the watchers on the bank.

"I am the fearsome green-crested, grey-necked, egg-eating monster," he repeated happily, proud of remembering his part. "I am—"

"*Egbert!*" shouted Sophie furiously.

Egbert shook the weeds out of his eyes and looked up. He saw Sophie, puffed up with anger, hanging over him like an avenging avalanche about to fall.

"Just a joke," he mumbled hastily.

Spinning himself round with one leg, he paddled away at top speed. What else could he do? He'd told Mirabelle that Sophie would recognize him, and she had. It wasn't his fault.

The wretched mud pack on his neck weighed him down. He began to feel dizzy.

The sun on the water dazzled him. A duck shrieked in his ear. A tiny moorhen swung across his vision like a mote in his eye.

Hector burst out from behind a clump of reeds. Hector, with his neck arched over his back, busking through the water in battle display. Hector, a cloud with an iron beak, so big and fierce and unforgiving.

Terrified, Egbert turned again and fled, praying that Hector would let him go.

Now Mirabelle was coming towards him, snorting and honking. What was she trying to tell him?

"Go away! Go away!"

Go away? Why? Where? Then he realized he'd turned full circle and was swimming straight back towards Sophie's nest. He could see her behind Mirabelle, spreading her wings. He could hear her calling Hector to protect their eggs. He tried to hide —

Too late. Hector was upon him, beating him with his heavy wings. There were feathers and beaks and legs and flying water everywhere. He lost his balance and toppled over. With the weight of mud on his neck, he sank to the bottom, dazed and defeated.

CHAPTER 8

William rushed up to Kitty and Jake. "She was going to hit me!"

"Who?" Kitty asked.

"The swan lady. She stood over me and lifted her big umbrella – "

"Why? What were you doing?"

"Nothing."

"She wouldn't just hit you for nothing," Kitty began. "You must've been up to something – "

"Hey, look over there!" Jake interrupted. "What are those swans doing? I think they're going to fight."

"No, they aren't," Kitty informed him, in

her most aggravating way. "Swans hardly ever fight, you know. They'll go on huffing and bluffing till one of them swims away. See, there he goes, the one with the funny neck. The big one won't follow him – "

"The big one is following him," Jake said gleefully. "So there, Miss Know-it-all! And here's another coming to join in!"

"Stop them! Stop them!" William shouted. "They'll hurt each other!" He jumped up and down on the bank, teetering over the water's edge. Jake caught hold of his arm. "Steady on," he said.

"Let go!"

"Can't. I promised Mum I wouldn't let you fall into the river."

"I can swim! I can!"

"Five strokes in a swimming bath," Jake said, shaking his head. "Not enough. Besides, why should you want to fall into the dirty old, muddy old river…"

"There's a swan lying on the bottom!" William was nearly crying. "It'll drown if we leave it there. Let me go!"

Kitty, too, had seen the swan go down. While her brothers argued, she slid down the bank into the shallow water between the rushes. Her feet sank into the moist mud, so deep that when she tried to lift them, they came out of her brand new shoes, leaving them stuck in the mud.

Mum'll kill me, she thought.

To her relief, the big male was swimming back to where his mate sat on her nest. The small pretty swan stayed where she was and hissed. The one at the bottom stirred feebly.

It's injured, she thought, for a cloud of what she took for blood was rising from its neck. It was a very odd colour. Did swans have brown blood? Was it dying, poor thing?

"Lift it up! It'll drown!" she heard William yell.

Could swans drown? She must remember to ask Dad. Jake was shouting now, telling her to come back and look after William. *He* would do it. He would rescue the swan.

She wanted to do it all by herself. Pretending she hadn't heard him, she waded a little nearer… Supposing the injured swan was too heavy for her to lift? Supposing the other swans attacked her?

Dad's right, she thought. *I should let Jake have a turn at being admired sometimes.*

But before she could call for him to come and help, she heard a loud splashing on her left. She turned her head and saw the swan lady striding towards her through the water. Her skirt was tucked into the elastic of her black cotton knickers. She was waving her big umbrella, and roaring at the top of her voice, "Shoo! Shoo!" Mirabelle backed away and hissed. Kitty stood her ground. For one thing, she was too frightened to move. For two things, her feet were stuck fast into the mud.

The swan lady thrust her umbrella at her. "Hold that!" she commanded.

Kitty was so surprised she nearly dropped the umbrella. She saw the swan lady roll up her sleeves and bend right down into the river so that her bottom was up in the air and her arms and face under the water. Her grey feather hat fell off and went floating away.

When she stood up again, she was cradling a swan; a live swan, a struggling, snorting, choking swan. Tucking him firmly under one arm and holding his beak in her other hand, she carried him to the bank.

The three children cheered.

*When the swan lady stood up, she
was cradling a swan.*

Mirabelle was confused. Her heart had nearly broken when she'd thought Egbert was dead. Now she saw he was alive but before she could rejoice, he was being carried off by that walking tree, or whatever it was. Where was it taking him? What was it going to do with him? Have him for its supper?

Mirabelle attacked, pecking and beating her wings.

"Keep that stupid bird off me," the swan lady bellowed. "She thinks I'm hurting her mate. Don't hit her. Just make a noise."

Jake and William shrieked and shouted and waved their arms about like windmills. Kitty opened the big umbrella and pumped it in and out so that it looked like a black swan flapping its wings.

Mirabelle retreated but only a little. She circled around, waiting to attack again.

"I won't hurt your precious mate," the swan lady said gently. She was sitting on a twisted root, with her feet in the water, holding Egbert firmly in her lap with one hand while she washed the thick mud off his neck with the other. "Don't you recognize your friend, you silly bird?" she asked. "Who feeds you wholemeal bread in the hard winter months, eh? Who nurses you when you're hurt? Who frightens away bad children when you're nesting, eh? Don't you recognize me?"

Perhaps the swan did recognize her, for she stopped hissing, though she did not go away.

"You put the mud on far too thickly," the swan lady went on. "It's a wonder he didn't drown, weighed down like that. Still, it's coming off now." She removed a large clot from Egbert's neck. He turned his head and pecked her feebly. "Ungrateful bird," she said, laughing and tapping his beak reprovingly.

"Can I help you?' Jake asked, sitting down beside her.

He'd expected to be snubbed. Instead she thanked him, and showed him how to hold the swan's beak and head while she washed its neck.

"You have good hands," she said. "Gentle and firm."

Jake went pink with pleasure.

"Can I help?" Kitty asked eagerly. "I'm very good at holding things."

The swan lady shook her head. "Where are your shoes?" she asked. "Hadn't you better find them and put them on? You don't want to cut your feet. People throw all sorts of nasty things into the grass."

Then she sent William to fetch her knitting bag from beside the bench, to bring it and put it on the grass behind her.

She's very bossy, he thought.

But he ran off to do as he was told.

She had saved the injured swam. Her dress was soaked and splashed with mud, her hair bedraggled, her little feather hat floating down river towards the sea, lost for ever. "Don't you recognize your friend?" she'd asked the swans.

She deserved a reward. She had done more than he had to help the swans.

The silver egg was a dream and it would probably never hatch, he thought, in spite of the magic charm he'd put on it. Probably the sad swan would tear away the silver paper, and say, like Kitty, "Look, it's only a trick!"

"I wish I could really do something to help the sad swan," he said to himself as he put the knitting bag down by the swan lady's side.

He must have spoken aloud, for she turned her head and smiled at him kindly.

"You already have," she said. "At least, I hope so. Wait and see."

Egbert and Mirabelle swam close together.

CHAPTER 9

Egbert's neck was still somewhat grubby, but it was bendy again.

He and Mirabelle swam close together, occasionally bumping softly against each other, turning their heads in unison to avoid seeing Sophie's nest.

"I'm sorry, Mirabelle," Egbert said.

"It doesn't matter, dear. It was a stupid plan. And dishonest," she added, as if this had only just occurred to her.

"Perhaps tomorrow we'll have an egg of our own," Egbert suggested.

"Perhaps. Tomorrow or tomorrow or tomorrow." Mirabelle sighed. "Never mind, dear. At least we still have each other."

"They look fond of each other,' Kitty said, watching them go.

"They are." The swan lady smiled. "Swans are loving birds. They mate for life."

Then she told them they were good kids, and said goodbye. "I must go back to my bench. I expect my skirt will dry in the sun." She looked at William. "I have two nests to keep my eyes on now."

"Do you really come here every day?" Jake asked.

"Only in nesting time. Since I've retired, I've nothing better to do. I love it here by the river."

"Even when it rains?" Kitty asked.

"I have my big umbrella," the swan lady said.

With that, she picked up her knitting bag

and went striding off over the grass without looking back.

"What a funny woman," Kitty whispered.

"Oh, I don't know," Jake said. "She certainly knows a lot about swans. Did you see how cleverly she handled that one? I doubt if I could have held its wings like that, even though she said I'd got clever hands. I expect she's an ornithologist."

"What's that?" William asked.

"A bird person," Jake told him.

A bird person? Was she half swan, half woman? Did those big black shoes contain webbed feet? Were there feathers under that bunchy dress?

William did not ask these questions aloud. He knew his brother and sister would have laughed at him.

* * *

"Egbert, look!" Mirabelle cried.

There was an egg in the once-empty nest.

"Where has it come from?" he asked, puzzled.

Mirabelle stood on the side of the nest and peered down at it. "Have you ever seen a more beautiful egg? Isn't it big? Isn't it handsome?"

"It's exactly like one of Sophie's," Egbert said.

Mirabelle hastily lowered herself over the egg, concealing it from prying eyes. "It's mine," she told him firmly. And then added kindly, "Ours."

"But how did it get there? Do you think Sophie gave it to us?"

"No. She wouldn't give us an egg-tooth, let alone an egg."

"Perhaps that peculiar angel put it in our nest."

72

"Which angel?"

"The one who saved my life. The one who feeds us in the hard times. The one with big feet. That one."

"Egbert, you're a genius!" Mirabelle said happily. "I never thought of her. An angel! Of course! What else could she be? And did you notice, she wore a feathered hat today? That must be the sign from heaven, so we'd know what to expect."

"But we didn't know what to expect," Egbert protested.

"Only because Sophie misled us. D'you know what she told me? That her eggs come from somewhere inside her. Have you ever heard of such a ridiculous idea?"

"It's beautiful!" William breathed.

CHAPTER 10

It was the second week of May. It had rained in the night. Drops of water still hung like crystals in the trees, and every leaf was newly washed. From behind a clump of reeds, two proud and happy swans came swimming into sight. Between them was a single cygnet. Small and fluffy and grey, it came out of the shadows, and the sunlight caught it, turning it into a bird of spun silver.

"It's beautiful!" William breathed. "Oh, it's beautiful!" He turned to the others. "It's magic after all, isn't it?"

The swan lady smiled slyly, thinking of the second egg, which she had picked up from the riverbank and slipped into the empty nest. But she said nothing.

It was Kitty who answered. Looking at William's glowing face, she swallowed the words she'd been going to say, and said instead, "Yes, it's magic."

"It always will be," William said happily.

And so it was. Even when he grew up and left his book of magic behind, the enchantment stayed with him. All his life, the silver swan glided through his dreams.

THE

END

THE OWL-TREE
Jenny Nimmo

The owl-tree is not like any other tree Joe has ever seen. It's huge and leafy and shivers at times like a person; it even seems to speak. Granny Diamond once saw an owl perched among its branches and has loved the tree ever since. It means the world to her. But her neighbour, Mr Rock, wants to cut it down. Why does he dislike the owl-tree so much? Does the tree have a secret to tell Joe? And how can he, a boy too scared even to *climb* the tree, be the one to save it?

MORE WALKER PAPERBACKS
For You to Enjoy